The Icky St...

Written by
Dawn Bentley

Designed and Illustrated by
Salina Yoon

On a pretty blue lake, on a big brown log
sat a very quiet little green frog.
A fly flew by.
SHH! Frog didn't make a sound.
He just eyed the fly flying around.

WOOP! Out came Frog's tongue
so sticky and long, and

SLURP! The fly was gone!

Just as Frog was swallowing the fly
a colorful beetle came crawling by.

SHH! Frog didn't make a sound.
He just eyed the beetle crawling around.

WOOP! Out came his tongue so sticky and long and

SLURP! Now the beetle was gone.

The frog swallowed the beetle
like he swallowed the fly,
then a green grasshopper
came hopping by.

SHH! Frog didn't make a sound.
He just eyed the grasshopper
hopping around.

WOOP! Out came his tongue
so sticky and long and
SLURP! Now the
grasshopper was gone!

Frog swallowed the
   grasshopper hopping by
like he swallowed the beetle
   and he swallowed the fly,
and then he saw a pretty butterfly.

SHH! Frog didn't make a sound.
He just eyed the butterfly flying around.
WOOP! Out came Frog's tongue
so sticky and long and...

GULP! The frog was gone!